Save Christmas

Gargoylz: grotesque stone creatures found on old buildings, spouting rainwater from the guttering. Sometimes seen causing mischief and mayhem before scampering away over rooftops.

e.co.uk

Read all the Gargoylz adventures!

Gargoylz on the Loose!

Gargoylz Get Up to Mischief

Gargoylz at a Midnight Feast

Gargoylz Take a Trip

Gargoylz Put on a Show

Gargoylz Have Fun at the Fair

Gargoylz Go to a Party

Gargoylz: Magic at the Museum

Gargoylz Make a Splash!

Gargoylz Ride to the Rescue

Gargoylz Make a Movie

Gargoylz Summer Fun

Gargoylz on the Go!

Gargoylz Save Christmas

Save Christmas

Burchett & Vogler
illustrated by Leighton Noyes

RED FOX

GARGOYLZ SAVE CHRISTMAS
A RED FOX BOOK 978 1 849 41185 1

First published in Great Britain by Red Fox,
an imprint of Random House Children's Books
A Random House Group Company

This edition published 2010

1 3 5 7 9 10 8 6 4 2

Series created and developed by Amber Caravéo

Set in Bembo Schoolbook

Red Fox Books are published by Random House Children's Books,
61–63 Uxbridge Road, London W5 5SA

www.**kidsatrandomhouse**.co.uk
www.**rbooks**.co.uk

Addresses for companies within The Random House Group Limited can be found at: www.randomhouse.co.uk/offices.htm

THE RANDOM HOUSE GROUP Limited Reg. No. 954009

A CIP catalogue record for this book is available from the British Library.

Printed and bound in Great Britain by CPI Bookmarque, Croydon, CR0 4TD

Happy Christmas to all Gargoylz fans everywhere.
– **Burchett & Vogler**

For June and Alwyn Crawshaw who are as warm and kind as they are inspirational, with love.
– **Leighton Noyes**

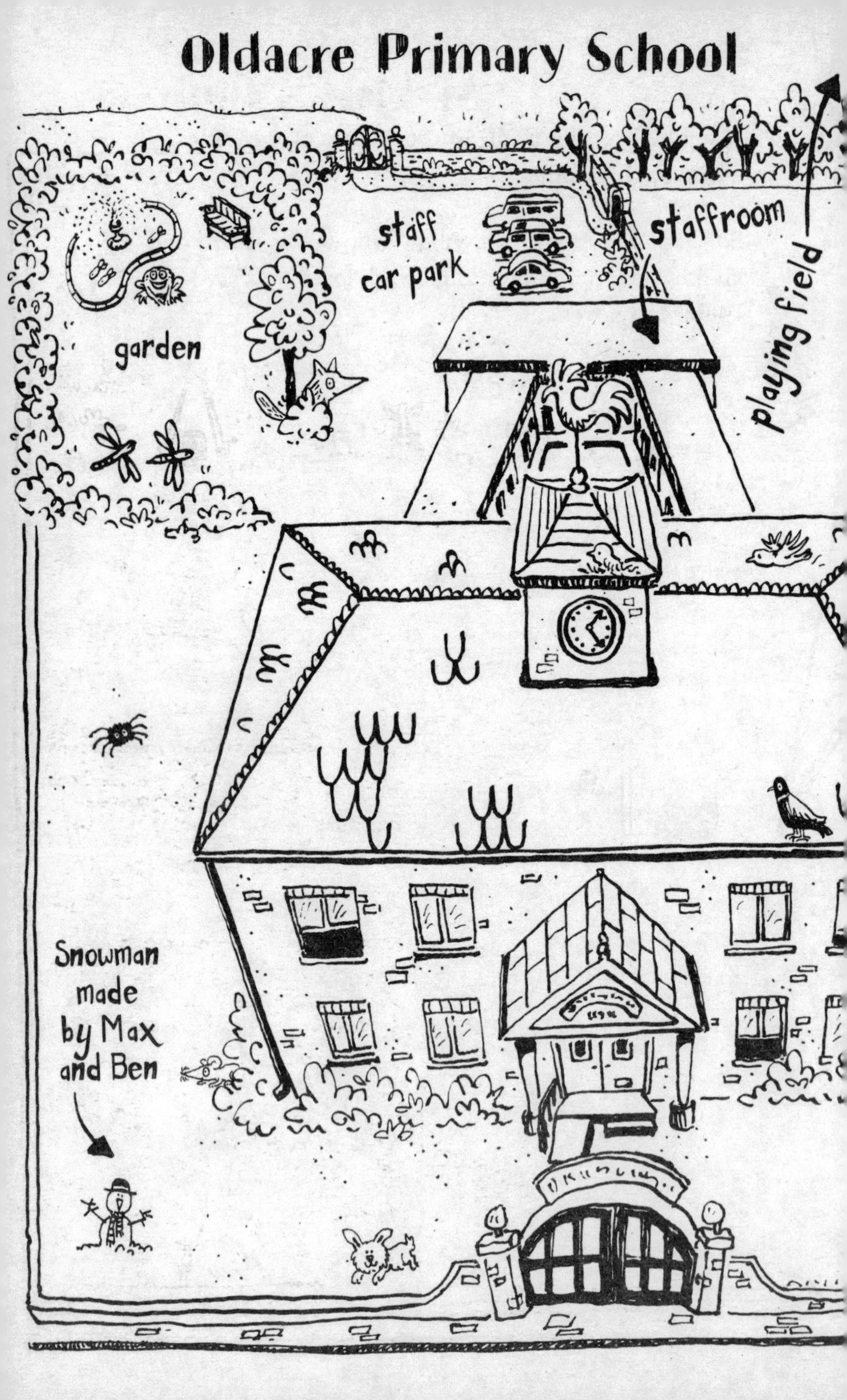
Oldacre Primary School
staff
car park
staffroom
playing field
garden
Snowman
made
by Max
and Ben

St Mark's Church

playground

School Report – Max Black

Days absent: 0

Days late: 0

Max is never afraid to make a contribution to history lessons. His demonstration of a battering ram using a broom and a bucket was very realistic, although the resulting hole in the classroom door was not ideal.
I worry that Max only seems to play with Ben Neal, but he assures me he has a lot of friends at the local church.

Class teacher – Miss Deirdre Bleet

Max Black's behaviour this term has been outrageous. He has repeatedly broken school rule number 739: boys must not tell 'knock knock' jokes in assembly. He is still playing pranks with Ben Neal. Mrs Pumpkin is absent again after the exploding paint pot incident. And Mrs Simmer, the head dinner lady, says the mincing machine has never been the same since he fed his maths test into it.

Head teacher – Hagatha Hogsbottom (Mrs)

School Report – Ben Neal

Days absent: 0

Days late: 0

This term Ben has been very inventive in PE. However, attempting to tightrope-walk across the hall was a little dangerous – and used up all the skipping ropes. He spends far too much time in class looking out of the window and waving at the gravestones in the churchyard. He would be better learning his spellings – a word he insists on writing as 'spellingz'.

Class teacher – Miss Deirdre Bleet

Ben Neal is always polite, but I am deeply concerned about his rucksack. It often looks very full – and not with school books, I am certain. It has sometimes been seen to wriggle and squirm. I suspect that he is keeping a pet in there. If so, it is outrageous and there will be trouble.

Head teacher – Hagatha Hogsbottom (Mrs)

Contents

1. Crisis at the North Pole

It was Christmas Eve. Max Black and his best friend, Ben Neal, were zooming through Oldacre Village on their imaginary superspy turbo sleighs.

"This is the last of Mum's Christmas cards to be delivered, Agent Neal," said Max. They screeched up to a large house with an inflatable Father Christmas in the garden. Max pulled a crumpled card from his rucksack and shoved it through the letterbox.

"Mission completed, Agent Black!" exclaimed Ben, revving his sleigh engine.

"Now we can get to the church and hand out *our* cards to the gargoylz. That's going to be much more fun!"

The gargoylz were the ugly stone statues that hung on the roof of the local church. Max and Ben had discovered that, when no one else was looking, the little creatures came to life. And even better, they loved to play tricks. As this was the very thing that Max and Ben loved to do most, they'd all become friends straight away.

The boys roared along the high street towards the church, dodging the last-minute Christmas shoppers. They dashed past their school and sped into the churchyard. Max skidded to a halt on the path. Ben piled into him, knocking them both into a heap among the gravestones.

They heard a burst of gurgly laughter from the roof.

Toby and Azzan were peeping over

the gutter. Toby, a cheeky, monkey-faced gargoyle, flew down to join the boys. All the gargoylz had a secret power, and Toby's was flying.

At that moment there was a tremendous cooing above them, and a bunch of pigeons poked their heads out beside Azzan.

"I've never seen that many pigeons on the church roof!" said Max.

"They're gargoyle Christmas cards," Toby explained.

"Are you sure?" asked Ben. "How would you stick them on the wall? They'd keep flying off."

"They're not that sort of card!" chuckled Azzan, letting out a burst of flame which sent the nearest pigeons flapping into the air in alarm. Azzan couldn't always control his special power.

Eli, Neb and Bart appeared on the church porch and came scampering down, followed by all the boys' other gargoyle friends.

"They've come with Christmas messages from our friends around the world," said Bart, straightening his gladiator skirt. "We speak pigeon, you see."

"We've got Christmas messages too," said Ben eagerly. "We've made you cards."

The boys tipped up their rucksacks and a pile of envelopes showered out.

The gargoylz rummaged through them eagerly.

Eli held up a large card with a drawing of a grass snake wrapped around a pot of itching powder. "That'sss me using my ssspecial power!" he exclaimed. "Thank you." All the snakes on his head tried to look at once and got themselves into a tangle.

"I drew that one," Max told him. "It's you playing that brilliant prank on Sports Day."

"And here's mine!" cried Jelly, flapping his pterodactyl wings in excitement. "It shows me turning into a gloopy ball, waiting to fool Barry Price – the big bully."

"And here's me – invisible!" Zack held up a blank card with holly round the edge.

Suddenly the pigeons on the roof started cooing loudly. Everyone looked up to see a bedraggled pigeon flying over the church. It plummeted down, bounced off the spire and landed on Bart's head with a flurry of feathers. It cooed feebly in his ear and then fell on its back in a bush.

"It's Percy!" shouted Cyrus, a fierce-looking gargoyle with lots of pointy teeth. He gently lifted the dazed pigeon out and propped it against a gravestone. "He's exhausted. Get him some food."

Bart gave Percy a handful of seed and a drink of fresh rainwater from a puddle. The pigeon quickly recovered. He puffed his chest out and looked solemnly at them with his beady black eyes.

"**Coo-coo**," he went.

"Shiver me timbers," squawked Ira, a parroty gargoyle who was convinced he was a fierce pirate. "That's a terrible tale."

"**Coo-coo-coo**," added the pigeon.

"How dreadful," exclaimed Barney.

The spiny ridges down his back quivered anxiously.

"**Coo-coo**," said the pigeon, flapping his wings. "**Coo-coo-coooo**."

"Of course we will," said Theo, with a swish of his stripy tail.

"What's the matter?" asked Ben. "That didn't sound like a Christmas greeting."

All the gargoylz started talking at once.

"It was a message from Ruben," said Jelly.

"He's a dear gargoyle friend of ours," said Abel, shaking his twiggy fingers. "In fact, as he looks like a reindeer, he's a *deer* friend. Did you like that pun?"

"Good one, Abel," chuckled Bart, who loved jokes.

"Ruben lives at the North Pole," Theo burst in.

"He needs our help," said Zack, popping anxiously in and out of view.

"What sort of help?" asked Max.

"We don't know," answered Barney. "But it's very urgent."

"Percy said Ruben will be arriving in about an hour," explained Toby. "Spluttering gutterz! We must be ready to go with him."

As he spoke, a faint jingling sound could

be heard. The air sparkled, and suddenly a gargoyle in the shape of a reindeer appeared in front of them.

"Ruben!" chorused the gargoylz, clamouring around him.

"How did you get here so quickly?" asked Max. "Percy's only just arrived."

A merry grin lit up Ruben's face. "Percy has to fly," he chuckled. "That's far too slow for me. I can go wherever I want – in the blink of an eye. It's my special power."

A big lumbering gargoyle with a warty face rubbed his hands together. "So you need our help," he said. "Do you want me to scare someone? I can turn into a terrifying skeleton."

"Thank you, Rufus," said Ruben, "but that won't be necessary."

"Need a sssnake?" said Eli hopefully. "I can turn into a nice ssslithery one."

"No thanks," said Ruben.

"Or a fierce pirate?" chirped Ira, slapping a wing over one eye.

"How about a tree?" suggested Abel. "I'm good at turning into trees."

"They're all great ideaz," said Ruben quickly. "But it's Santa who needz our help."

The gargoylz gasped with shock, and Jelly melted into a gloopy purple puddle on the spot.

"We must go to him immediately!" Neb swivelled his long nose about in the air. "Which way's north?"

"Can we come too?" asked Max. "We'd love to help Santa."

Ben nodded. "It would be a great way to thank him for giving us such cool presents every year."

"That's right," said Max. "That animal-noises box I got in my stocking was the best. I hid it in the bathroom, and every time Mum lifted the toilet seat it mooed at her."

"And the fishing rod was ace," said Ben. "When I found my bossy sister Arabella eating my bag of sweets I hooked them up and ran away before she knew what was happening."

The boys suddenly realized that Ruben wasn't listening. He was looking at them with an expression of horror on his reindeer face. "You're not gargoylz," he said. "You're humanz! Hide, everyone! Humanz mustn't see gargoylz under any circumstancez." He disappeared in a sparkly cloud.

"I hope he hasn't gone back to the North Pole without us," said Azzan.

"It's OK, Ruben," called Toby.

"Max and Ben are our friendz."

Ruben reappeared in a shower of glitter. "Why didn't you say so in the first place?" He held out a hoof for the boys to shake. "Pleased to meet you. Of course you can help Santa. The more the merrier."

Max and Ben high-fived in delight.

"How do we get there?" asked Ben. "We haven't got your special power."

"We'd have to catch a bus to the station," said Max, "then the train to the airport, then—"

Ruben shook his antlers. "No need for that, boys," he laughed. "You'll be travelling with me."

The gargoylz gave a big cheer.

Theo jumped onto Ruben's head and hooked his claws around his antlers. The others tried to climb on behind.

"We don't all fit!" complained Bart as he slid off and landed on his bottom. "I don't want to be left behind."

"No problem!" said Ruben. "As long as you're touching me, you'll share my special power."

Max and Ben managed to get a grip on the gargoyle's stony tail.

"Close your eyes," ordered Ruben, "and off we go for a merry ride!"

Everyone closed their eyes.

"Nothing's happening," said Max, disappointed.

"Is this a gargoyle trick?" asked Ben.

"Open your eyes," came Ruben's voice.

The boys obeyed.

The churchyard had vanished. In its place was a pure white landscape, dotted with fir trees covered in glittering snow. Above them in the dark sky shone a bright winter moon and millions of twinkling stars.

"We're at the North Pole," gasped Max. "Awesome!"

"But I don't feel cold," said Ben.

"That's part of the magic of Santa's kingdom," Ruben told them. "Come on. Time to meet the man himself."

"Are you sure we're in the right place?" asked Ben, puzzled. "There's no sign of him."

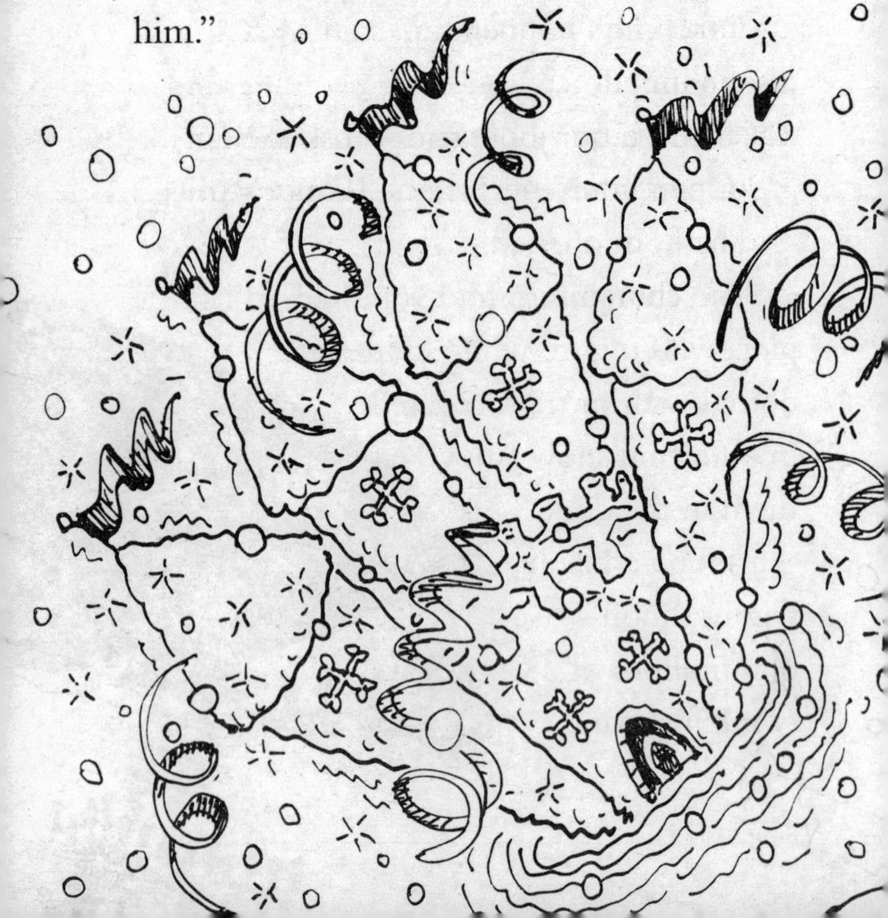

"Only very important people can see Santa and his grotto," said Ruben. "Now, look behind you."

Max, Ben and the gargoylz turned to see a circle of snow glittering and shimmering with magic. Then, to their utter amazement, the towers of a white sparkling castle rose slowly from the ground. They watched open-mouthed as the magnificent castle grew taller and taller. Twirling ribbons shot into the air from its turrets, exploding like magical fireworks and showering them all with golden sparks.

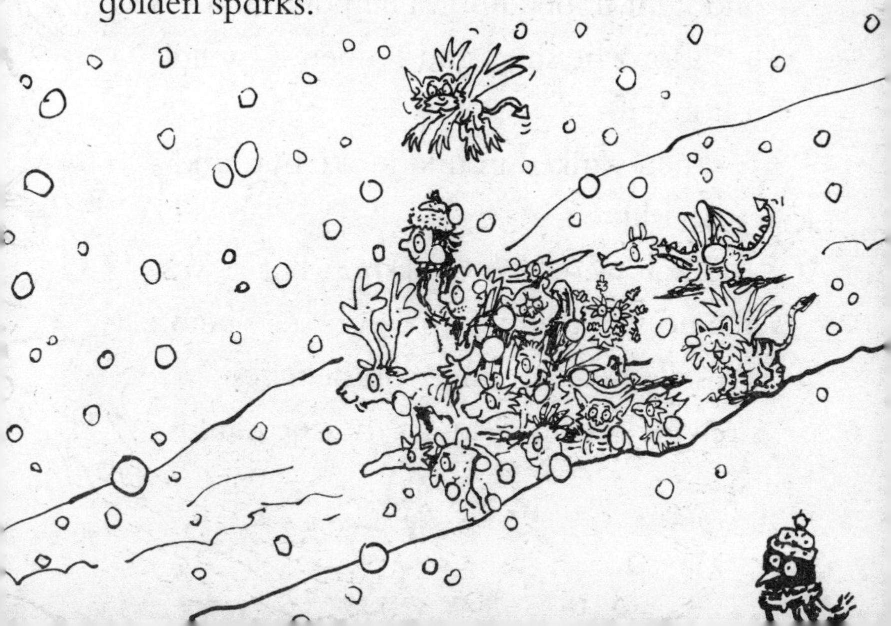

"Wait till you get inside," said Ruben. "Your eyez will pop out on stalks." He trotted off across the snow. Max and Ben and the gargoylz followed eagerly.

"This is the most awesome adventure in the history of most awesome adventures," declared Max.

As they walked up the steps of Santa's castle, the huge front doors swung open and light flooded out. They all hung back.

"Don't be shy," said Ruben, waving a hoof.

They walked in and looked around curiously.

They were in a workshop, but it was like no workshop they'd ever seen before. Tinselled shelves and workbenches stretched away as far as the eye could see. They were stacked full with every game and toy in the world, from pirate ships and train sets to brightly painted rocking horses. At one end of the room, a huge musical box with moving figures was playing jolly Christmas music while model racing cars whizzed about the floor. Helter-skelters and slides twisted down from the shelves. In the middle stood an enormous Christmas tree, stretching up to the ceiling. It was laden with sugar canes, silver bells and flickering candles.

Someone was sitting under the branches in a cosy armchair. He had a pile of half-finished toys next to him, and he was peering closely at a remote-control car with a loose wheel.

Max activated his spy radar. Long white beard, red jacket and trousers, kindest face in the world. He knew what that meant.

"It's Santa!" he gasped.

Santa looked up and his face broke into a merry grin. "Well, bless my boots! If it isn't Max Black and Ben Neal," he boomed, heaving himself out of his chair. He had a deep voice that sounded like chuckles and scrumptious chocolate all mixed together. "And Ruben's friends, the

Saint Mark's gargoylz. Welcome to my grotto." He flung out his arms to greet them.

Max and Ben were almost bowled over in the rush to reach Santa. The jolly old man staggered back into his chair, covered in boys and gargoylz.

The gargoylz tried to show him their special powers – all at the same time. Bart burped some massive spiders while Zack became invisible and ran around with Santa's glasses. Jelly melted into his boots and Abel did his best to turn into a Christmas tree.

"Ho, ho, ho," laughed Santa as he watched their antics. Then he turned to Ruben with a worried frown. "I usually love to see visitors," he said, "but we're really behind with making the presents because of the poor elves. I don't know how we're going to be ready to deliver them all tonight."

"That's why my friendz are here," explained Ruben. "They've come to help."

"Bless my boots, how kind," said Santa, his round face lighting up.

"What's wrong with the elves?" asked Max, looking around the workshop. A few tired-looking helpers with pointy ears and bells on their hats were sitting at a workbench, hammering and gluing.

"They're not well," sighed Santa. "Most of them have got the dreaded Sneeze Disease."

"Is that bad?" asked Ben.

Santa nodded. "Elves hate sneezing," he said. "It upsets them and they have to go to bed."

"Only a few elves are well enough to work," Ruben told them. "And that's not enough to make all the presents and get them wrapped. There'll be a lot of disappointed children around the world this Christmas."

Max and Ben threw off their coats. "Not if we can help it!" they cried.

There was a loud slurping noise, and suddenly the two boys found themselves covered in green slime.

"Help!" yelled Ben.

"What's going on?" spluttered Max, trying to fight his way out.

They heard a burst of gargoyle laughter.

"I detect joke slime, Agent Neal," said Ben with a grin.

"Brilliant prank, gargoylz," exclaimed Max, peeling the gloopy goo off his face.

The gargoylz popped up from behind a toy rocket.

"It was Jelly's idea," said Eli. His snakes gave a giggly hiss.

"I haven't laughed so much since Zack dropped an ice cube down the vicar's back and he squealed all through the Sunday service," added Toby.

Santa rubbed his hands together happily. "I see the gargoylz have found the box of tricks and pranks for mischievous children's stockings."

"You have a whole box?" gasped Max.

"You should see it," said Neb, his nose twitching happily. "Fake soap, plastic spiderz—"

"Let's keep the rest a surprise," said Santa, with a big, beaming smile. "I'm going to put an extra helping of tricksy toys into your stockings as a special thank-you gift for helping me."

"That's awesome!" gasped Max. "How did you know that would be just what we wanted?"

Santa's eyes sparkled. "It's my job to know," he said.

"Just think of it, Agent Black," sighed Ben happily.

"We'll be able to play tricks all year, Agent Neal," mused Max.

"And we all love playing tricks!" yelled the gargoylz.

2. The Extra Elf

Santa beamed at Max and Ben and the gargoylz.

"Time to get to work," he told them, beckoning to an elf who was scurrying by. "Tinsel here will give you your jobs."

"Hello, hello," said the elf in a squeaky voice. "Delighted to meet you."

"Greetingz!" said Toby. "We're the Saint Mark's gargoylz, and this is Max and Ben."

"We're going to have so much fun," chirped Tinsel. "Come with me."

He led them to a row of high shelves

stacked with all sorts of toy parts – jigsaw pieces, plastic sword handles, flashing robot eyes and a pile of batteries. An elf in a green jacket sat at a table with a long list and an old-fashioned feather pen.

"This is Holly," said Tinsel. "He's in charge of the parts department. What he calls for – we get. Then we dispatch it to the toymakers' bench. Look, we'll show you."

Holly checked his list. "Yellow buttons for walkie-talkie."

Tinsel dashed up a nearby ladder and scrambled along a shelf. "Got them!" he cried. He jumped to the ground and gave a whistle. A little wooden

steam train came speeding out of a tunnel, smoke puffing merrily from its chimney. It gave a cheerful **whoo-whoo** and chuffed to a halt next to Tinsel. He popped the buttons in one of its trucks and it set off towards the workbench.

"We can do that!" yelled Barney. "Gargoylz are good at climbing. I'll go and get the next thing."

"Stop right there!" said a croaky voice. Another elf came marching across the floor, clutching a clipboard. He peered over his half-moon glasses at them.

"My name is Sprout and I am your safety officer," he told them. "There'll be no work from you visitors until I've told you the first 'elf and safety rule."

"That's a good pun!" said Abel. "He really meant *health* and safety."

Sprout gave him a stern look. "As I said, 'elf and safety rule."

"That sounds boring, Agent Black," whispered Ben.

"Agreed, Agent Neal," Max whispered back.

"Then there will be the official tour of Santa's grotto." Sprout looked down at his clipboard. "Now, 'elf and safety rule number one. Visitors must never climb the warehouse shelves . . ."

Max and Ben and the gargoylz

groaned. Sprout cleared his throat and continued.

"... when they can use a jet pack instead!"

He gave them a twinkling smile as he took a box from under the table and handed out shiny jet packs.

"Awesome!" cried Max.

The boys and gargoylz quickly strapped them on.

"Just what a superspy secret agent needs," gasped Ben. He pressed a button, shot to the ceiling and whizzed around the star on top of the Christmas tree.

"Goodnesss!" hissed Eli, the snakes on his head wriggling with excitement. "Thisss will be fun."

"It's making me fly even faster than usual!" said Toby, doing a speedy lap of the grotto.

"Nose-cone for alien rocket ship, money for toy post office, bales of hay for model farm," called Tinsel. "Four dolls' legs, thirty-two building bricks, seven teddy-bear ribbons."

Whoosh! The boys and gargoylz were off, flying all round the shelves to find the required toy parts and drop them in the train trucks. Soon the shelves were half empty.

"Watch this for superspy jet-pack skill!" cried Max as he looped the loop.

"I wish we could have jet packs in our stockings," Ben yelled back, scooping up a pair of fluffy rabbit ears. "But I expect they're top secret."

At last Sprout tapped on the table. "Attention, please! It's time for your tour. Follow me."

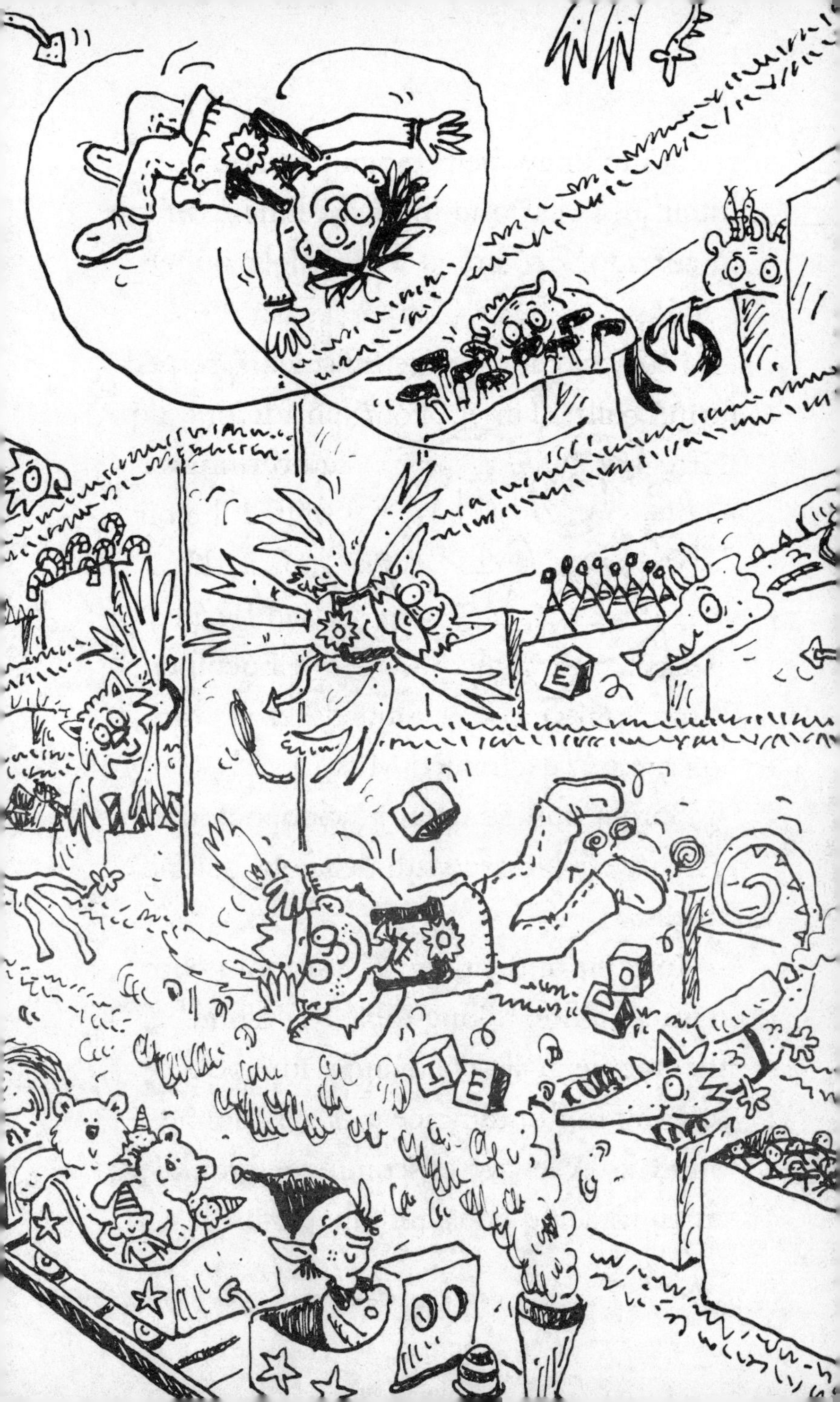

Santa's new helpers whipped off their jet packs and followed him down a corridor decorated with bright paper chains.

"What's that wonderful smell?" gasped Neb, his long nose quivering as it sniffed the air.

"Cookiez!" cried Barney.

"Chocolate," sighed Azzan.

"Cake!" exclaimed Max.

Sprout pushed open a wooden door. They were blasted with delicious baking smells.

In front of them lay a vast room with a roaring fire. A long table ran along the middle. It was heaving with cookies and muffins and mince pies, all cooling on racks. A few elves scampered around carrying icing bags and huge bars of chocolate. They were all wearing face masks.

Someone was standing at the table decorating fairy cakes.

Max's spy radar leaped into action: big rosy cheeks, apron covered in hearts, and white hair with silvery sparkles. He knew what that meant. It was Mrs Santa.

"Come in, come in," she cooed.

Sprout picked up a white face mask from a basket and snapped it over his mouth and nose.

"Do we have to wear those?" whispered Ben. "Is it more 'elf and safety?"

"They're just for the elves," said Ruben, shaking his stony antlers. "And only when they're in the kitchen. They love chocolate, you see."

"Just like gargoylz," said Barney, licking his lips.

"But if elves smell it, they can't stop themselves eating it," explained Ruben. "There'd be none left for the cakes."

"They can always tell when it's nearby," called Mrs Santa, dropping sprinkles onto the icing, "and they can't control themselves. So I've made them mint-scented masks."

Max picked up a mask. "It's wonderful," he said, inhaling the fresh smell.

Mrs Santa beamed. "Polar mint. It's the only thing that

will block the whiff of chocolate from an elf's nose."

"We all get chocolate after work," said Sprout. "That's 'elfy eating."

The gargoylz gathered around Mrs Santa, their tongues hanging out.

"Do you need masks as well?" she chuckled. "Now, I need help packing the cookies up into gift boxes."

"All crew reporting!" squawked Ira.

"Wait a minute," said Sprout severely. "Don't forget 'elf and safety rule number two. No handling cookies" – the gargoylz' faces fell – "until you've tested one first!"

"A most important rule," laughed Mrs Santa, passing round a plate of gooey chocolate-chip cookies.

"How could we have thought 'elf and safety would be boring?" whispered Max.

Ben grinned. "Nothing's boring in Santa's grotto."

They set to, arranging the cookies in bright red boxes.

Mrs Santa went by with a tray of mince pies. "Just test these for me, boys and gargoylz," she said, handing them out.

"Dangling drainpipes," said Toby, wiping the crumbs from his mouth. "I haven't had so much fun since the vicar thought Abel was a Christmas tree and stuck a fairy on his head!"

"They're scrumptious!" spluttered Barney with his mouth full.

"I've got a recipe joke," said Bart, with a deep gurgling chuckle. "What does an elf use to make himself fly?"

"I don't know," chorused his friends. "What does an elf use to make himself fly?"

"Elf-raising flour!" he told them.

All the gargoylz rolled about the floor, chortling loudly. The elves joined in.

After they'd tested and packed the cookies, cupcakes and brownies, Sprout called for them to continue the tour. He dropped his mask in a bin by the door and led them up some winding wooden stairs into an enormous loft room. Triple bunk-beds lined the walls, covered in bright quilts and squashy pillows. A little elf hat could be seen on each pillow. And loud sneezes were coming from every one.

"This is the room for un-'elfy elves," said Sprout. "Everyone here has the Sneeze Disease."

"It's . . . **atishoo** . . . horrible," said a voice in the nearest bed. A red nose poked out from under the covers.

"It's . . . **washooo** . . . miserable," sneezed another elf.

Four elves with flashing blue lights on their hats scurried about giving cough medicine and anti-sneeze drops to the patients.

"There's something fishy going on here, Agent Neal," said Max, taking Ben aside.

"I agree, Agent Black," agreed Ben. "It's very odd that nearly all the elves should get the Sneeze Disease at the very same time. *And* at such a critical time of year!"

"Highly suspicious!" hissed Max.

"It reminds me of the trick I played on Arabella," said Ben. "I put sneezing powder on her scarf and she sneezed all the way to school."

"That served her right for being an annoying sister," said Max. "Do you think someone's playing a prank like that here?"

"It's possible," said Ben. "Let's see what the gargoylz think. They're master tricksters, after all."

He asked the gargoylz to gather round and told them about their suspicions.

"I'll investigate," said Toby. He flew over to the nearest bed and sniffed hard at the pillow.

"**ATISHOOOOO!**" Toby sneezed so hard he turned three and a half somersaults, crashed into the wall and slid to the floor in a heap. "Spluttering gutterz!" he groaned as he struggled to his feet. "That pillow's full of pepper."

The other gargoylz gasped.

"That's terrible!" exclaimed Ben.

"Really nasty!" agreed Max.

"I'll tell you what it is," said Sprout, shaking his head crossly and making the bell on his hat clatter. "It's a matter of 'elf and safety. It's stopped the elves getting on with their important work." He scratched his nose. "But I can't think of anyone here who would do such a mean thing."

"How about gnomes?" said Ruben thoughtfully. "They're always up to mischief."

"But no gnomes work here," said Sprout. "Only you and the Santas and us elves. One hundred and fifty-seven elves, to be precise. We'd know at once if there was anyone else."

"Perhaps you'd better do a count," suggested Ben.

"Good idea!" Sprout produced a bright shiny whistle and gave a sharp blast. All the elves in bed sat up, the nursing elves stood in a line and, from far away, footsteps could be heard approaching fast.

"Everyone will be here in a jiffy," Sprout told them.

Soon the room was bursting with elves. Sprout and Ruben walked up and down counting.

". . . one hundred and fifty-six . . . one

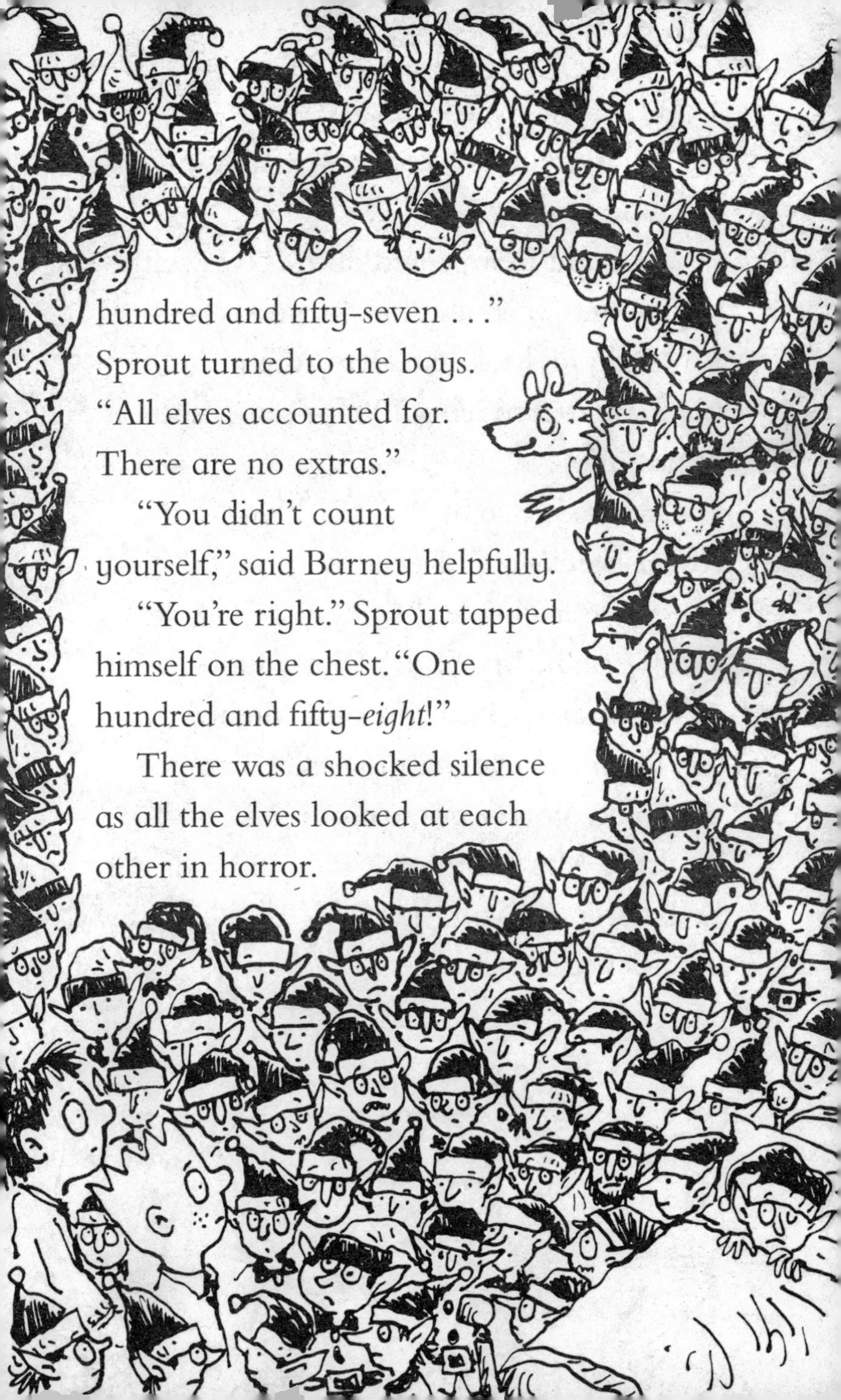

hundred and fifty-seven . . ."
Sprout turned to the boys.
"All elves accounted for.
There are no extras."

"You didn't count
yourself," said Barney helpfully.

"You're right." Sprout tapped
himself on the chest. "One
hundred and fifty-*eight*!"

There was a shocked silence
as all the elves looked at each
other in horror.

"That means someone here isn't a real elf," said Ruben.

Max and Ben peered at the elves, with their pointy ears and bright, perky hats.

"They all look like elves, Agent Neal," muttered Max. "Which one is the impostor?"

"We need Secret Plan: Elf Test, Agent Black," said Ben.

"You're right! And I've got a brilliant idea!" cried Max. "Back in a minute."

He dashed off towards the kitchen.

"Could I have the most chocolatey chocolate you've got, please?" he asked Mrs Santa as he burst in. "It's an emergency."

"I've got just the thing," she said. "Here – Polar Cocoa Delight."

Max stuffed the big silver-wrapped bar in his pocket, shouted thank you over his shoulder and dashed back to the bedroom.

"I've got chocolate," he whispered to Ben. "And the elves are not wearing their minty masks. Watch them closely."

Max had barely finished speaking when, nose twitching, Sprout and all the other elves dived at him and began to pull at his pocket. Max was knocked to the floor in the rush.

"Chocolate!" they all chanted. "Lovely chocolate."

"Help!" cried Max. "I'm being squashed. It's bad for my 'elf."

"Good pun," laughed Abel.

Rufus and Bart waded in and pulled the elves off. Barney helped Max to his feet.

"We want chocolate," cried the elves, reaching out their fingers. Ben rushed over, grabbed the battered chocolate and quickly threw it out of a window. The elves immediately stopped jabbering.

Max pulled down his jumper and re-spiked his hair. "Anything to report, Agent Neal?" he asked.

"I have, Agent Black," replied Ben. "Secret Plan: Elf Test is a success! That elf standing by the triple bunk-bed only moved *after* he saw all the others jump on you."

"No elf should be able to resist Polar Cocoa Delight," said Ruben, shaking his antlers. He strode over to the quivering elf and pulled off his hat.

There was a shocked gasp around the room as the elf's pointy ears came away too.

He stood there looking frightened. And now Max could see that he wasn't an elf at all. He was round and plump, with short, tufty hair and tiny ears like cup handles.

"He's a gnome!" shouted Sprout angrily. "Send for Santa."

An elf scurried out.

"A gnome?" said Toby, puzzled. "But where are his red cheeks and pointy hat – and his fishing rod? I know all about gnomes. The vicar's got them in his garden as ornaments. This one doesn't look anything like a gnome. He hasn't even got a beard."

The gnome frowned. "I most certainly *am* a gnome!" he snapped. "And I'm *not* a garden ornament!"

"What's going on here?" boomed a voice, and Santa strode in. He peered down at the gnome, who scowled back at him.

"He put pepper in our pillows!" said Tinsel.

"Why did you do that?" asked Santa.

"'Cos I was angry," muttered the gnome. "I wanted to work here with you and make toys and pack cookies, but you only let elves do that. That's why I made the elves ill – so I could be a helper."

"What's your name?" asked Santa kindly.

"Gnigel," said the gnome sullenly. "It's not fair, you know. I could be just as good an elf as the elves."

"Well, Gnigel," said Santa. "Anyone can work at my grotto as long as they're cheerful and they work hard. Would you like to be my first gnome helper?"

Gnigel's eyes lit up. He ran around in delighted circles. "I'm going to be a helper! I'm going to be a helper!" he chanted, waving his stubby arms in the air. "I'll be the best employee you ever had," he said, jumping up and down in front of Santa.

Then he stopped and looked guiltily at the elves. "I'm sorry for the trick I played on you," he said, shuffling his feet. "It was mean to make you all think you had the Sneeze Disease. I'll make it up to you all, you see if I don't." He looked around the room. "First I'll wash all the elves' pillows and get rid of the pepper."

"Then you can make them some hot chocolate to speed their recovery," said Santa. "Then I think you'll settle in very nicely."

Gnigel gave a huge grin. "Yes, sir," he declared, scuttling away to gather up the pillows.

Santa beamed at Max and Ben. "Thank you, boys," he said. "You used your experience as expert tricksters to solve a nasty elf health scare. Now let's get back to work and make this a Christmas that everyone will remember."

"Hooray!" yelled the elves.

"Hooray!" cried the gargoylz.

"Hooray!" shouted Max, high-fiving Ben. "I never thought work could be so much fun!

3. Gargoylz and Gift-wrapping

Santa rubbed his hands together and beamed at his crowd of eager helpers.

"Max, Ben and the gargoylz can get to work wrapping the toys that are ready," he said. "My elves will finish making the last ones, now they're fit and healthy again."

"I think Santa means fit and *'elfy,*" Abel whispered to Bart.

"We need a superspy plan of action, Agent Neal," said Max, "so that we can work double quick."

"We do indeed, Agent Black!" answered Ben. "Gather round, everyone. I've thought of something brilliant."

Max, Ben and the gargoylz got into an excited huddle and Ben told them his idea. Barney edged towards the kitchen door. "I'll check whether Mrs Santa needz any help with the cooking," he said with a cheeky wave. "See you later."

At last Ruben held up a hoof for silence. "That is a perfect plan," he announced.

"Placez, everyone, and let's get going."

Zack popped into view. "What's the plan? What's the plan?"

"Weren't you listening?" asked Toby.

Zack shook his head. "I was exploring," he said. "Trying out the roller skates."

"I'll go through it again," said Ruben. "Your job is to take a jet pack—"

"That's all I need to know!" cried Zack. He strapped the nearest one on his back and pressed all the buttons at once. Immediately he spun off around the workshop like a balloon losing its air.

When his friends had finally got him down from the top shelf and told him exactly what he had to do, they all took their positions.

Bart read out the presents from a long curling list. Max, Zack and Rufus whizzed over to the workbench where elves were doing their final checks, collected the toys and slid them to the other end of a long shiny table, where Toby, Eli and Azzan wrapped them up.

"Thisss is sssuper fun!" said Eli, carefully folding red shiny paper round a toy garage.

"I love wrapping presents," said Azzan, letting out a burst of flame in his excitement and sending his paper up in smoke.

Toby wrapped it again, then jet-packed

up and placed it at the top of a helter-skelter. It zoomed down and shot off at the bottom onto another table, where Theo, Abel and Neb were ready with the ribbon.

"We're the best gargoylz for this job," said Neb, "because we've got long fingerz and clawz."

"We're Santa *Clawz*!" chuckled Abel.

"I'm the one with the best tiger clawz," Theo insisted. He pounced on a ball of ribbon, overbalanced and fell in the waste-paper bin.

Ben and Jelly were waiting on a small quad bike with a basket on the back. They piled in the presents and sped off to Cyrus. Cyrus was hanging upside-down from a trapeze. He grabbed the presents and swung over to Ira, who was perched on a rope swing. Ira collected them in his beak and sailed over to a huge brown sack.

"There she blowz!" he cried, dropping the presents into the sack.

"This is going brilliantly!" declared Ruben as he ticked them off on another list. "We're sure to be ready in time."

Just then, Santa appeared and beckoned to Max and Ben. "I've got something very special I want your help with," he said. He led them over to two scrolling lists that reached from the floor to the ceiling of the grotto. One had the heading NICE, and the other one NAUGHTY.

"Here are the names of every child in the world," explained Santa.

Max looked at the names, written in curly gold handwriting. "But there are millions of children in the world," he said, puzzled. "I can't see millions of names."

"And I can't see ours," added Ben. "Or anyone we know."

"I should have told you – they're magic," said Santa. "Call out the name of any place in the world, and new 'naughty' and 'nice' lists appear. Between them they'll have the names of every child who lives there. As you two live in Oldacre, you can choose presents for all the children you know." He winked at them. "See if the magic lists work for you."

"Oldacre Village!" shouted the boys together. For a moment the lists flickered, then some familiar names appeared.

"There's Gavin," cried Max, pointing to the top of the

"nice" list.

"And Duncan," added Ben.

"And us!" yelled the boys together.

"*Phew!*" exclaimed Max. "We're on the 'nice' list too."

"But so is Barry Price," said Ben. "And he's always horrible to us."

"I know," said Santa with a twinkle in his eye, "but he's kind to his old gran. Make sure you choose a really good present for him and all the others. But don't forget – you must double-check the list."

"We've got a problem here, Agent Black," said Ben when Santa had gone. "Barry can't have anything he could bully people with."

"Good thinking, Agent Neal," replied Max, looking around the piles of toys in the workshop. "There's a great cricket bat here, but he'd whack everyone with it."

"And a cool science kit," said Ben. "But he might try and blow us all up."

"How about this!" suggested Max, picking up a shiny black go-kart helmet with red flames on. "The colours match his favourite go-kart. And it's much more streamlined than his old one."

"Brilliant!" exclaimed Ben as Max gave it to the wrapping team. "Who's next?"

The boys quickly worked their way down the list.

"What about this princess board

game for Jessica," said Max. "As long as I don't have to play it with her."

"Only Lucinda Bossy Boots Tellingly left now," said Ben. "She's not going to be easy."

"There's a box of joke make-up," suggested Max. "When you put it on, your face goes green."

"I'd love to see her wearing that!" laughed Ben. "But Santa wouldn't be too pleased. He might take us off the 'nice' list. There's a brew-your-own-perfume kit here."

"Bleugh!" said Max. "It smells all horrible and girly. It ought to come with nose pegs. She'll love it."

Holding the smelly box at arm's length, the boys jumped on skateboards and took the last of the Oldacre presents for wrapping.

A bell sounded. "Attention all helperz!" cried Ruben. "Santa's sleigh is packed and ready to go!"

Everyone gave a big cheer, and Mrs Santa came bustling out of the kitchen with biscuits and hot drinks. Barney trotted along behind carrying a tray of shortbread, his face covered in crumbs.

"Work's not over yet," announced Ruben when they'd finished their snack. "It's time to harness up the reindeer. And that could take a while. They can be very mischievous."

"They sound like our sort of reindeer," whispered Max.

Ruben led the way towards a small door at the back of the grotto. It had a sign, TO THE STABLES.

Everyone burst outside to see a wonderful sight. There in the deep snow stood Santa's sleigh, piled high with the huge sack of presents. It sparkled all over with swirly golden magic, and right at the front was a long bench seat with soft, velvety red cushions.

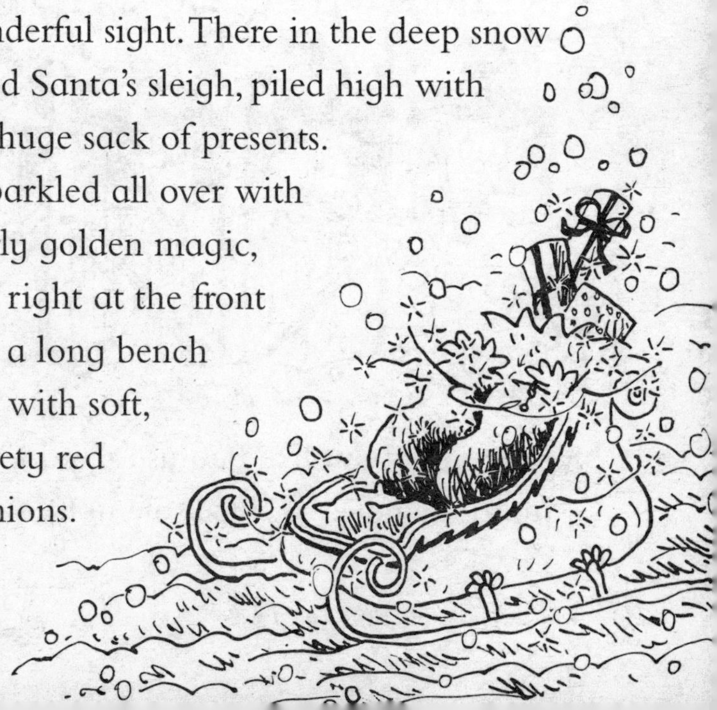

"Bounce on the cushionz! Bounce on the cushionz!" declared Zack, but before he could dive into the sleigh, Ruben held up a hoof.

"No time for fun," he told the disappointed gargoyle.

Ruben trotted up to a line of nine stable doors. Eager-looking reindeer were poking their noses over each one. "Listen up," he told them firmly. "It's Christmas Eve. This is our most important night of the year.

No messing about like you usually do."

Santa's reindeer nodded solemnly.

"No time for fun," agreed Zack.

Ruben opened each stable door in turn and the reindeer trotted out and stood in a straight line, staring at the boys and gargoylz.

"They don't look very mischievous," whispered Ben, disappointed.

All of a sudden he was splattered on the head with a big wet snowball. He turned to see the reindeer at the far end of the line give a merry wink to the others, scoop up

another hoof-full of snow and toss it at Max with his antlers.

With that, all the reindeer began to caper around in the snow, rolling snowballs with their hooves and flicking them expertly at the boys.

"Stop!" cried Ruben, but they took no notice. The other gargoylz' eyes lit up with delight.

Zack nudged Ruben. "Time for fun now?" he asked.

"Well . . ." said Ruben with a grin. "Just a few minutes then."

"Into battle!" yelled Toby, and everyone scooped up handfuls of snow.

Soon the air was full of white flying missiles.

Ira flapped his wings and a flurry of snowflakes fluttered down over them all. "This is even better than making it rain!" he squawked in excitement.

"It doesn't feel wet when it goes down your neck," yelled Ben as a warm snowball splatted on the back of his head.

"It's magic," agreed Max, kicking up a snowflake blizzard at Abel, who quickly turned into a tree and shook it off his branches.

"Right, down to work," called Ruben at last. The fight stopped and everyone waited for their instructions. Ruben fetched a pile of jingling harnesses out of the stables and handed a list to Toby.

"That's the order the reindeer go in when they pull the sleigh," he explained. "They have to go like that – otherwise they don't pull straight. One year we had terrible trouble and got stuck on top of Mount Everest."

Ruben tried to grab the nearest reindeer, who hopped out of the way, making him fall face first in the snow.

The other deer snickered and ran around in circles. By the time Max and Ben and the gargoylz had managed to harness them all, three reindeer were facing the wrong way and one was upside-down!

Suddenly they heard a clock chiming from inside the grotto.

"It's time to go!" announced Ruben in a panic, "and we're still not ready. What's Santa going to say?"

The reindeer immediately stopped

mucking about and trotted into two neat lines. Toby checked the list. "Dasher, Dancer, Prancer, Vixen, Comet, Cupid, Donner and Blitzen. Everyone's in the right order," he reported to Ruben. "Wait, there's one missing."

A reindeer with a bright shining red nose took his place at the front of the line.

"It's Rudolph!" gasped Max.

"That's right," said Ruben. "He leadz the sleigh. His nose is very useful when it's foggy."

The door to the castle opened and Santa came out into the snow, followed by Tinsel, Holly and a small team of excited elves. He beamed when he saw the

sparkling sleigh with the reindeer hitched up and ready to go. The elves hopped into the sleigh, the bells on their hats jingling merrily.

Azzan tugged at Santa's coat. "Can we help deliver the presents please?" he asked. "We'll be good."

"Of course you can!" declared Santa. "Hop aboard."

Grinning with delight, the gargoylz scrambled into the sleigh.

Max stepped forward. "May we come too?" he asked.

"I'm sorry," said Santa solemnly, "but I can't take boys on my sleigh."

The boys' faces fell. The gargoylz looked shocked.

"On the other hand," Santa went on, stroking his beard, "if I work a teeny bit of magic . . ." He waved a hand over Max and Ben's feet. They felt their toes tingle and looked at their feet. Their trainers had turned into curly green elf shoes!

Now Santa waved his hand over the boys' heads.

"Dangling drainpipes!" cried Toby. "He's turned you into elves!"

The boys looked at each other and burst out laughing. They'd both grown a pair of long, pointy ears.

"And elves are definitely allowed to help," said Santa with a happy smile. "Just for tonight you'll be able to fit down chimneys – that's elf magic. But don't try it when you're human again. You might get stuck!"

"Thanks, Santa!" gasped Max and Ben.

"Don't mention it," said Santa, patting them both on the head. "It'll be fun having you two along . . ." He turned away to look for the gargoyle reindeer. "Ruben will take you home now," he went on.

"But we're coming with you, aren't we?" said Ben.

"You've got to go to bed first," said Santa. "Otherwise your families will be out looking for you."

"I'll pick you up again when everyone's asleep," Ruben assured them.

Max and Ben looked at each other.

"We can't go home like this though," said Max. "We can hide the shoes but everyone will notice the ears!"

"No they won't," Santa told them. "Only a few young children can see elf magic."

"Awesome!" cried Max.

"Sizzling snowballs!" exclaimed Santa, with a wink at the boys. "I haven't had so much fun since Azzan breathed fire over the vicar's Christmas tree and all the baubles melted."

"How did you know that?" gasped Azzan.

"It's my job to know," said Santa. "And I know this is going to be . . ."

". . . the best Christmas in the history of best Christmases!" yelled Max and Ben.

4. 'Twas the Night Before Christmas

Max burst in through his front door.

"You haven't been gone long," called his mother. "Did you deliver all my cards?"

"Of course, Mum," Max called back. He didn't tell her that he and Ben had also been to the North Pole and back in the blink of an eye. Or that they'd be helping Santa with his deliveries that night.

Mum and Jessica were in the kitchen making mince pies.

"Can I have my tea?" Max asked eagerly. "I want to get to bed really early."

"I know it's Christmas Eve," said his mum in surprise, "but it's not even five o'clock."

"I just can't wait for Santa to come," answered Max.

"Max has got pointy ears!" exclaimed Jessica suddenly.

Max gulped. Santa had said that some young children could see the elf magic.

"Of course he hasn't, Jess," said Mrs Black.

"It's true," insisted Max's sister.

"I don't think Santa wants to hear naughty things like that," her mother told her.

Jessica humphed crossly. "Pointy shoes as well," she muttered when their mother's back was turned.

As soon as Max and Jessica had eaten their tea and got their pyjamas on, they put out a snack for Santa.

"Carrots for the reindeer," said Jessica, placing them under the Christmas tree. "And a mince pie for—"

"One's not enough," burst out Max. "Don't forget the garg— I mean, the elves. They *love* mince pies."

Jessica stared at him. "How do you know that?" she demanded.

"Everyone likes mince pies, don't they?" Max said quickly. He piled the plate high.

"I still think you've got funny ears," said Jessica. She looked down at Max's feet. "And your slippers have gone all pointy. I'm telling Mum you're playing a trick on me."

"You're just getting over-excited about Santa coming," Max told her. "Hang up your stocking and get to sleep quickly or he won't bring you that princess game."

"How do you know I'm getting that?" asked Jessica suspiciously. "My letter to Santa was top secret."

"Just a guess," blustered Max. "But if you really want it, you'd better go to bed now or maybe Santa won't come."

Jessica gave a cry of alarm and was in bed with the light out in seconds.

Max dived into his own bed and pulled up the covers. His mum came in to say goodnight and he closed his eyes.

A second later he heard **jingle, jingle!** He opened his eyes to see

Ruben standing in his bedroom.

"Ready?" asked the gargoyle, lowering his head so Max could touch his antlers.

"You bet!" cried Max.

Ruben blinked, and Max found himself in Santa's sleigh, which was parked up on his roof. He found himself perched on a cushion next to Santa, who was holding the reindeer reins.

Ben appeared on the other side. Max could see that his friend's pyjamas had turned into a bright green elf suit, and looked down to see that his own had been transformed too. The boys gave each other an excited thumbs-up.

"Good to see you again, Max-elf and Ben-elf," said Santa.

"We can't wait to get going!" exclaimed Max in excitement.

He looked down over the side of the sleigh. Oldacre was spread out far below them. Lights were dimming all over the village as mums, dads and children went to bed.

"Greetingz!" came a voice, and Toby and the other gargoylz sprang up from behind Santa's sack.

"Giddy-up," cried Santa, shaking the reins. Ruben hopped into position at the front of the sleigh just like the figurehead on a ship.

The boys felt a tremor of magic go through the sleigh.

"Hold on," cried Ruben.

Max and Ben grasped the rail as the sleigh zoomed off the roof with a super-fast **whoosh**. Soon Max's house was just a tiny dot below them.

"This is awesome!" cried Ben.

"Double awesome," yelled Max.

Rudolph, his nose glowing brightly, led the way through the starry night.

To the boys' astonishment, they suddenly found themselves over a vast, sprawling city. Theo pointed at a tall tower down below.

"I'd love to climb that metal thing!" he cried. "It's even higher than the steeple on the church."

"That's the Eiffel Tower in Paris," said Toby. "I've seen it on Max's television. We're flying over France."

"How did we get here so quickly?" gasped Max. "Paris is miles away from Oldacre."

“It was Ruben,” said Bart. “He blinked.”

Mountains, deserts and oceans sped by beneath them.

At last Santa brought the sleigh down to hover over some red tiled roofs in a town by a lake.

“Ben-elf and Max-elf, you can come with me for our first delivery,” he said. “With the gargoyle-elves, of course.”

He grabbed his sack and a list, hopped off the sleigh and jumped down the nearest chimney with a **whoosh**.

The gargoylz followed.

"Here goes," cried Max. He jumped over the side of the sleigh, and felt himself tingle as Santa's magic **whooshed** him down the chimney. He tumbled into the fireplace and landed among the gargoylz.

Ben landed beside him. "That was as good as a fairground ride!" he exclaimed.

A pretty Christmas tree stood in the corner of a cosy lounge and three red spotty stockings hung above the fireplace.

"Ho, ho, ho!" cried Santa as he checked his list, delved in his sack and handed the gargoylz a pile of presents. "Ben-elf and Max-elf, you fill the stockings."

The gargoylz formed a line and passed the presents along from paw to paw. At the end of the line the boys took them and quickly stuffed the stockings to bursting.

"Bless my boots!" cried Santa. "You all did an expert job. Off we go." He strode over to the chimney.

"Her-rum!" coughed Ruben, tapping him with his hoof. "Snack time, sir!"

"Of course!" Santa grinned. "Let's see what the children have left us." He peered down at a plate under the Christmas tree. "Cookies for us and green beans for the reindeer."

"That's jolly kind," said Jelly, poking excitedly at the plate with his long pterodactyl beak.

"It is indeed," said Santa. "Tuck in, everyone!"

"Spluttering gutterz!" gasped Toby, showering crumbs over them all. "These are delicious. I like helping Santa."

Santa picked up the beans for the reindeer and ushered everyone to the fireplace.

Zoom! Before they could say "crackers", they were sucked up the chimney and back into the sleigh. The reindeer happily tucked into their beans.

Santa and his team delivered present after present, filling stockings, shoes, or whatever the children had put out ready for his visit. Even where there were no chimneys, Santa's magic **whooshed** them into every house, flat, bungalow, tent or caravan where children were sleeping.

At each stop there were delicious snacks for everyone.

"We must have been all over the world by now," said Max at last. "I wish this could go on for ever. But the sack's nearly empty."

"We're not quite finished yet," said Santa.

"Ruben – you know where we're going next."

They flew over fields and roads. Suddenly Ben pointed ahead. "That's Barebones Castle!"

"We're nearly home!" cried Max. "There's Oldacre in the distance."

Santa beamed at them all. "We've got a few towns and villages left before we get to yours. But first I have an important announcement to make. Max-elf, Ben-elf and gargoyle-elves, you are now fully trained helpers. That means you can do deliveries on your own."

Max and Ben high-fived and the gargoylz let out a whoop of joy as they whisked down the chimney of a small cottage. Max and Ben followed their gargoyle friends and helped them fill the bright embroidered stockings while Barney inspected the little tray by the fireplace.

"Mince piez!" He sighed with pleasure

and crammed them into his mouth.

"Leave some for us," grumbled Rufus.

Suddenly they heard a gasp at the door. A small boy stood there with a glass of milk in his hands. He gawped at them, open-mouthed.

"We've been seen!" squeaked Barney, the spines on his back quivering. At once he turned to stone, a terrified look on his face.

"Don't mind us," said Max quickly. "We're Santa's helpers."

"Mummy!" cried the little boy. "Santa's elves are here!"

"I'll scare him back to bed before his mum comes," whispered Theo. "I'll use my secret power and turn into a fierce tiger.

Then we can make our escape."

He wriggled his stony bottom and became a sweet little stripy kitten. Theo always thought he could turn into a terrifying tiger. However, as he was a young gargoyle, just four hundred and twelve years old, he could only manage a kitten, however hard he tried.

"**Grrr!**" he purred.

"Here, kitty kitty," called the little boy, bending down and offering Theo the milk.

Then he ran towards the stairs. "Mummy,

Mummy!" he yelled. "Santa's elves have got a cat!"

"Time to go," said Barney.

They rushed to the chimney and **zoom!** they were back up in Santa's sleigh.

"Did something go wrong?" asked Santa, with a twinkle in his eye.

"We were seen . . ." began Max.

". . . by a boy!" added Ben.

"But I turned into a tiger and he ran off," said Theo proudly.

Santa threw back his head and roared with laughter, his huge belly shaking. "I knew it would be fun having you along," he said, wiping the happy tears from his eyes.

"But if children see us, it'll spoil your

secret," said Max.

The gargoylz gathered around, their stony faces looking anxious.

Santa thrust his hand into his pocket and pulled out a small pot.

"Is that bubblez?" asked Toby. "We like bubblez."

"You blow it just like bubbles," Santa explained. "But it's actually magic sleep powder. Guaranteed to put any child to sleep in an instant . . ."

"Like when I use my special power and sing," put in Cyrus.

". . . and when they wake up, they just think they've had a lovely dream," said Ruben.

Max and Ben and the gargoylz jumped down the next chimney and into a room where a huge pile of mince pies, cookies and Christmas cake had been left.

"I can't manage any more food," groaned Max.

"Nor can we," chorused the gargoylz.

"I can!" declared Barney. While the others tiptoed through the house, filling ten stockings at the feet of ten beds, he tucked in.

By the time his friends got back there wasn't a crumb in sight.

"Time to go," he said, with a wistful look at the empty plate.

He went over to the fireplace. **Zumph!** He disappeared.

"That didn't sound right," said Max.

"Help!" came Barney's muffled voice.

Max peered up the chimney. Two little stony legs were waggling above him.

"I'm stuck!" wailed Barney. "I've eaten one too many mince piez!"

"We'll soon get you out," Max assured

him. The boys gave him a shove but Barney was stuck fast.

"We'll help," said Theo and Rufus. They put their hands on Barney's stone bottom and pushed hard.

But Barney still didn't budge.

"I'll be stuck here until next Christmas!" he cried.

"So will we!" said Bart gloomily.

"Look out!" called Barney. "I've let out a pong. Sorry."

Everyone quickly held their noses and

flapped the smell away. Barney's special power could be fun – unless you were right behind him.

Jingle! Jingle! Ruben appeared. "Having trouble?" he asked.

"Barney's jammed fast," said Ben.

"No problem! Grab hold of me, everyone." Ruben reached up and put a hoof on Barney's tail.

He blinked, and in an instant they were

all sitting on the sleigh again. Barney looked a bit sooty.

"I'll never eat another mince pie," he promised. "At least not for ten minutes."

Now they were flying over Oldacre. The sleigh landed on a roof near the church.

Santa whispered something to Cyrus, Azzan and Ira, and they jumped off the sleigh.

Max suddenly had a warm excited feeling inside. "I think they're going to our houses!" he whispered to Ben.

"Toby, Jelly and Eli can do the vicar's stocking," Santa went on. "And Max, Ben, Neb and Rufus can deliver to this house."

"I know who lives here," said Max as they scooped up the last few presents.

"The Basher," exclaimed Ben. "Cool! He can't do anything to us while he's asleep."

They **whooshed** down the chimney onto Barry's bedroom carpet.

"This is awesome," whispered Ben as they crept towards the huge stocking that Barry had hung at the foot of his bed.

Suddenly the bedclothes heaved and Barry sat up and rubbed his eyes. Max and Ben threw themselves out of sight and Neb used his secret power to camouflage himself, blending in with a football on the floor. But Rufus was too surprised to move.

"What's going on?" demanded The Basher, looking in astonishment at the horrified gargoyle. "Who are you?"

"**Miaow!**" said Rufus gruffly. "Don't mind me. I'm just a cat."

"Oh no," hissed Max. "He's trying the same trick as Theo."

"You can't be a cat," said Barry. "Cats don't have warts on their noses."

"Santa's cat does," insisted Rufus, trying

to edge towards the chimney.

"So where's Santa?" demanded Barry, looking around the room. "*He's* supposed to come tonight, not his cat." He caught sight of Ben's pointy elf slipper. "There's someone behind my wardrobe. Maybe that's him."

He got out of bed and marched towards the boys' hiding place.

"Time for the sleeping powder!" whispered Max urgently.

Ben fumbled in his pocket for the pot. He yanked open the lid just as Barry was staring down into their dark corner. The powder spilled all over Barry's legs.

"That's funny," said The Basher, scratching his head. "My knees have gone to sleep."

As he bent down to inspect them, Ben took his chance. He flicked some of the sparkling powder right up Barry's nose.

Barry immediately curled up on the carpet and began to snore.

Max prodded him to make sure he was properly asleep.

Neb stopped looking like a football and helped the boys cover The Basher with his duvet. Then they all filled his stocking with toys, the shiny red and black go-kart helmet at the top.

"I'd love to see The Basher's face in the morning," laughed Max when they were safely back in the sleigh.

"What happens now, Santa?" asked Ben. "Your sack's empty."

"You go to bed . . ." said Santa.

The boys' faces fell.

"Ho, ho, ho" – Santa chuckled – "after a Christmas party at the North Pole."

"Hooray!" cried Max and Ben together.

Santa flicked the reins and the sleigh shot off into the black night.

"I could blink us there in a second," Ruben called from his place at the head of the reindeer. "But we always take the long way home. It's pretty with the starz and the moon shining on everything. How's your tummy, Barney?"

"It feels a bit full for a party," said the little dog-faced gargoyle sadly.

"Come up here and make yourself comfortable," said Ruben. Barney scampered over the front of the sleigh and settled down between Ruben's antlers. "You can enjoy the view and soon you'll be hungry again. Mrs Santa will be making all sorts of lovely thingz for us."

Toby scuttled up to sit at the front with the boys. "I liked being an elf," he chortled. "I haven't had so much fun since we filled the vicar's crackerz with tinsel and his Christmas pudding got covered in glitter."

"It's been awesome," agreed Ben as the sleigh touched down in the gleaming snow outside Santa's grotto. "No one would believe it if we told them."

"I've just got one thing to say," cried Max. "Merry Christmas, gargoylz. Merry Christmas, everyone!"

Gargoylz Fact File

Full name: Tobias the Third
Known as: Toby
Special Power: Flying
Likes: All kinds of pranks and mischief – especially playing jokes on the vicar
Dislikes: Mrs Hogsbottom, garden gnomes

Full name: Barnabas
Known as: Barney
Special Power: Making big stinks!
Likes: Cookiez
Dislikes: Being surprised by humanz

Name: Eli
Special Power: Turning into a grass snake
Likes: Sssports Day, Ssslithering

Full name: Bartholomew

Known as: Bart

Special Power: Burping spiders

Likes: Being grumpy

Dislikes: Being told to cheer up

Full name: Theophilus

Known as: Theo

Special Power: Turning into a ferocious tiger (well, tabby kitten!)

Likes: Sunny spots and cosy places

Dislikes: Rain

Full name: Zackary

Known as: Zack

Special Power: Making himself invisible to humanz

Likes: Bouncing around, eating bramblz, thistlz, and anything with pricklz!

Dislikes: Keeping still

Full name: Nebuchadnezzar
Known as: Neb
Special Power: Changing colour to match his background
Likes: Snorkelling
Dislikes: Anyone treading on his tail

Name: Azzan
Special Power: Breathing fire
Likes: Surprises
Dislikes: Smoke going up his nose and making him sneeze

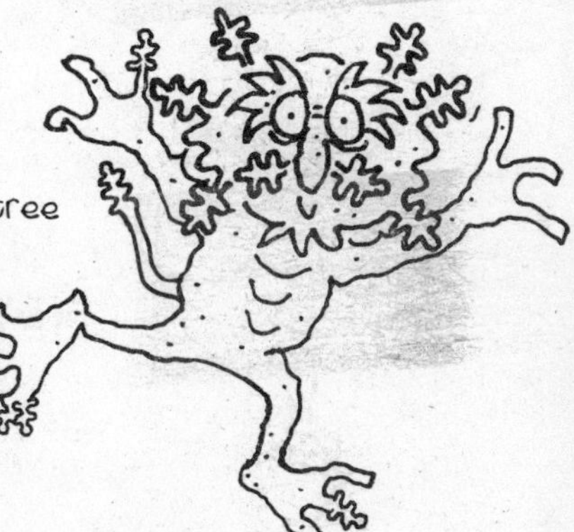

Full name: Abel
Special Power: Turning into a tree
Likes: Funny puns and word jokes
Dislikes: Dogs weeing up against him

Name: Ruben
Special Power: Can go anywhere in the world in a blink of an eye
Likes: Mrs Santa's baking
Dislikes: Delivering Christmas presents to houses where there aren't any snackz for Santa and his reindeer

Full name: Jehieli

Known as: Jelly

Special Power: Turning to jelly

Likes: Having friendz to play with

Dislikes: Bulliez and spoilsports

Name: Ira

Special Power: Making it rain

Likes: Making humanz walk the plank

Dislikes: Being bored

Name: Cyrus

Special Power: Singing lullabies to send humanz to sleep

Likes: Fun dayz out

Dislikes: Snoring

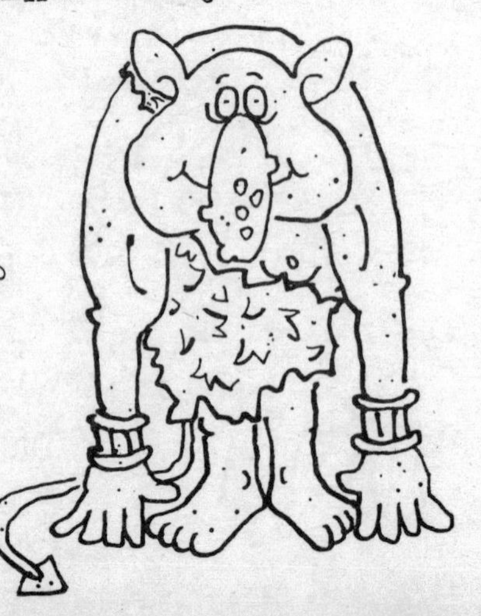

Name: Rufus

Special Power: Turning into a skeleton

Likes: Playing spooky tricks

Dislikes: Squeezing into small spaces